DID HOLLYWOOD CAUSE THE CUBAN MISSLE CRISIS?

And Other Alternative History Stories

John Corral

ISBN-13: 9798764063751
ISBN-10: 1477123456

Cover design by: Art Painter
Library of Congress Control Number: 2018675309
Printed in the United States of America

A reputation, once developed, is as valuable as a fine sword. But don't forget that it has to be a valid reputation. Or the sword's edge is no finer than a blunt object.

ERIC KOENIG, THE WAR OF 1812: WHEN HISTORY LIED

CONTENTS

PREFACE

These stories are historical fiction. Some are satire and others profoundly serious. Yet they are all plausibly written with historical facts and events used as the basis for more speculative narratives and alternative accounts of how history might have played out. They provide probable explanations for events or situations that might otherwise be perplexing. Some may call these conspiracy theories, implying falsification or sinister motives. They are neither. Rather, they are reinterpretations of history.

DID HOLLYWOOD CAUSE THE CUBAN MISSILE CRISIS?

In his newly published memoirs, Khrushchev's son-in-law finally revealed the origins of the crisis that might have led to full-scale nuclear war.

Sasha got up quickly as his father-in-law entered the room. It was his habit, even though his father-in-law, Nikita Khrushchev, the Soviet Premier, had told him numerous times that was not necessary.

"Always you sit," Khrushchev said, also out of habit. Then he went to a desk in the front room of his suite at the Waldorf-Astoria in New York, sat and put three spoonfuls of sugar into his tea and stirred… and stirred… and continued stirring for seemingly forever.

Khrushchev was disturbed about something and Sasha could see that he was troubled far more than usual. Sasha was a favorite of his, the son-in-law of his oldest daughter, Rada, and always in such situations Sasha found it better to let him get to whatever he wanted to say to him. They were alone, which meant Khrushchev wanted Sasha's opinion on something important. In due course his father-in-law would say what that was. He always did.

"Did I do right? Was what I did right?" Khrushchev finally said, in English, as was his way when asking about something having to do with the United States.

"Of course," Sasha replied, "Perfectly!"

"Why you not say that to Rada? She say you speak of good, not perfect. Was it good or perfect?"

Sasha looked at his father-in-law's eyes, studied them and knew he wanted honesty, not agreement as he got from his lackeys and grovelers otherwise, and from him too most times. "It was both," Sasha said, "perfect for all but the KGB. For them it was good."

"Why only good for them?"

"They did not come up with it; your plan for visit to West Coast of the United States. It was what they wanted, but not something they first proposed. That's why."

"I am Premier, I can do anything —even kill millions of Ukrainians like Stalin— but KGB wants to propose visit Hollywood first?" Khrushchev chortled.

"Only if it is the United States."

Khrushchev laughed loudly, threw his hands up, pounded them on the desk, and said, "They are like children, spoiled. Maybe they need lesson? I tour farms, I tour factories, I tour government buildings with old fat men because they want. And I must still do more of what they want?"

Sasha was quiet. He did not say anything in opposition to that, but his disagreement was obvious. He had accompanied Khrushchev to America when the Soviet Premier was invited by President

Dwight Eisenhower to a meeting at Camp David in July, 1959. The two countries were at loggerheads over another crisis in Berlin, the worse since the Cold War started.

The meeting was successful because within hours of meeting with Eisenhower a memorandum of understanding issued jointly by the two heads of state ending that crisis. The rest of the visit, scheduled to take ten days, was being taken up by hastily arranged tours; a farm in Maryland, the Newport News shipyards in North Carolina, and a session of the Senate Foreign Relations Committee in the Capital.

"What is it you think? What is it right to do?"

Sasha thought for a moment, and then said, "Give them what they want."

"And what that?"

"The KGB wants missiles on the United States, as they have on the Soviet Union. We are surrounded by hostile missiles, in West Germany, in France, in Great Britain, in Italy —all facing us. Meanwhile the United States has none in Canada or Mexico facing them."

"We have submarines with missiles… Nuclear missiles."

"Yes, but they have their own subs that track ours. We can't get within range without being stopped."

"How else to get missiles on United States?"

"There is Castro. The KGB loves him."

"Cuba? They are primitive, Indians, and welcomed Trotsky."

"That was Mexico."

"Same food, language… Everything."

"Cuba has Castro and he hates the United States."

"I am not going to trust nuclear missiles to primitive Indians."

"We would control the missiles, not the Cubans."

"The United States would not like missiles in Cuba. If they found out, they would do something serious… Like invade Cuba. We have invested billions of rubles there, in equipment, and have engineers there teaching those Indians."

"What if they only find out later, after missiles are there. The United States would not be in any position to do anything about them. You do not talk back to nuclear missiles. You simply accept them, as we needed to accept them from NATO."

"What else?

"Well, Shelepin always said he wanted to visit Hollywood. Have him come along. And his deputy, Semichastny said he wanted to meet Marilyn Monroe. Maybe we can get both?"

"That is good, and I want visit with Marilyn Monroe. She is very healthy woman, I know," as he made a circling motion with both his hands. Then, thinking a moment, he said, "Nina wants visit to Disneyland. That I will ask for. To make my wife happy too."

Two days later, Khrushchev and his entourage were in the air flying to Hollywood where Twentieth Century Fox was the winner in the contest to host them. The studio was filming the biggest movie in Hollywood then, *Can-Can*, starring Frank Sinatra and Shirley MacLaine, and promised the State Department they would have Marilyn Monroe there, who was a contract star with them, as well as most of Hollywood. They would have Khrushchev watch the filming of the movie, and first have lunch at the commissary, enhanced by elegant upgrading to *Café de Paris*, and sit among the biggest stars in Hollywood. When word got out, nearly everyone in Hollywood wanted to be there. It would be a turn-out only eclipsed by the Oscars.

Lost on most, the irony was that Hollywood was still in the grips of the "red scare," the investigations by Congress, the House Committee on Un-American Activities, which began investigating the movie industry, inspiring a blacklist of supposed communists that was still enforced in 1959. Stars and movie execs who were scared to death of being seen having coffee with a communist screenwriter were desperate to be seen dining with the communist dictator.

And what a turn-out it was! Of course, Frank Sinatra and Shirley MacLaine were in the forefront, plus others in the film, Maurice Chevalier and Louis Jourdan; Juliet Prowse and Marcel Dalio. But also Tony Curtis and Janet Leigh; Dick Powell and June Allyson; Elizabeth Taylor and Eddie Fisher; Gary Cooper and Kim Novak; Dean Martin and Ginger Rogers; Kirk Douglas, Jack Benny, and Zsa Zsa Gabor; on and on, legions more of equal fame. And, of course, Marilyn Monroe. The studio made certain she was there, and on time, assigning a trio of people to insure that.

Marilyn sat at table 8, just behind the front table where Khrushchev was sitting. At the same table was Henry Fonda and Debbie Reynolds; Producer David Brown and Director Walter Lang, both associated with Can-Can; and studio execs. One of the stars there, Edward G. Robinson, was heard to say, "I hope my funeral draws half the crowd."

Noticeably absent were Bing Crosby, Ward Bond, Adolphe Menjou and Ronald Reagan, who all turned down their invitations as a protest against Khrushchev. Also absent was Marilyn's then husband, Arthur Miller, urged to stay home by the studio because he had been a communist party member who had been investigated by the House committee and therefore was considered too controversial to dine with a communist dictator. His only part in the visit was to tell Marilyn who Khrushchev was and inform her, as best he could, what he was doing in this country.

"What if he asks me about America, what do I say?" Marilyn said to her husband.

Miller thought for a moment, and replied, "Wear the white, clingy dress you had on for your last movie premier, and he won't care what you say."

Exceeding the number of Hollywood celebrities that day at Fox studios were hundreds of police and other security people, including over two dozen Soviets. They feared the worse, that someone might attempt to harm the Premier, as someone had tried at the Maryland farm days earlier. Someone in the crowd had thrown a tomato at the Premier, but missed by several feet. Khrushchev was unfazed, and said, "A Russian would throw cabbage, and hit target."

There were incidents of booing when Khrushchev's motorcade made its way onto the lot at Fox studios, and many people at the entrance held signs denouncing the Soviet leader. But when the motorcade stopped in front of the commissary, the crowd there lightly applauded when Khrushchev emerged from his limo and shook hands with the studio head, Spyros Skouras. A few moments later Skouras led Khrushchev into the commissary, and the stars there stood to applaud.

"Which one is Khrushchev?" Shirley MacLaine was heard to say as the two men walked to the head table. Both were fat and balding, and no more than inches over five feet.
"The guy with the bad suit," said Frank Sinatra. "The other guy signs your check each week."

Khrushchev took a seat at the head table. At an adjacent table, his wife, Nina, sat between Bob Hope and Gary Cooper. And various other members of the Russian delegation were scattered through the commissary, each with their own interpreters.

Nina Khrushchev showed Frank Sinatra and Gary Cooper pictures of her grandchildren and said they had seen western movies, like she, and wanted to be cowboys. "You are a cowboy star, I have seen you in Man of the West and They Came to Cordura," she said to Cooper. And she added that her husband must also feel the same.

"He talks of bad Indians all the time now."

Charlton Heston attempted to make small talk with Mikhail Sholokhov, the Soviet novelist who would win the Nobel Prize in Literature in 1965. "I have read excerpts from your books," Heston said.

"Thank you," Sholokhov replied. "When we get some of your films, I shall not fail to watch some excerpts from them."

Midway through the lunch —squab, wild rice, and peas with pearl onions— the police chief approached the head of the U.S. delegation, Henry Cabot Lodge, and informed him that the Secret Service and he had concluded it would not be wise to go Disneyland as Khrushchev had requested, and this was communicated to the Premier. *What else could go wrong,* Khrushchev thought to himself.

Over dessert, Skouras stood up to speak. With a gravelly voice and a thick Greek accent, he also sounded a lot like Khrushchev.

Khrushchev listened to Skouras for a while, then turned to his interpreter and whispered, "Why interpret for *me*? He needs it more."

Skouras may have overheard Khrushchev, and appeared to change his prepared talk. Instead of a warm and friendly welcoming speech, it became somewhat of lesson in capitalism, using himself as the central focus.

"I may sound funny," he said, "but I am serious about what I am about to say. I am the classic American success story. Son of a Greek shepherd, I immigrated to America at 17, settling in St. Louis, where I sold newspapers, bused tables and saved my money. With two brothers, I invested in a movie theater, then another, and another, until by 1932 I was managing a chain of 500 theaters. A decade later, I was running 20th Century Fox."

Then, turning to the Premier, he said "In all modesty, I beg you to look at me, I am an example of one of those immigrants who came to this country because of the American system of equal opportunities. I am now fortunate enough to be president of this studio because of hard work, and the capitalist system."

Hearing that, Khrushchev could not resist heckling. "And maybe because you exploit workers. All your women are skinny —except for one maybe— because you serve them skinny birds."

That got a laugh from the audience.

"But they don't finish what we serve them now." Responded Skouras.

That got a bigger laugh.

When Skouras sat down, Lodge stood up to introduce Khrushchev. The ambassador talked about America's supposed affection for Russian culture, mentioning literature, ballet, art, stage and music, without mentioning movies.

Khrushchev shouted out, "What about our movies? Have you not seen *They Fought for Their Homeland?* It is great movie, based on great novel by Mikhail Sholokhov, and has great star Vasily Shukshin from Soviet theater."

"No," Lodge said, a bit taken aback.

"Well, you should see it," said Khrushchev. "We are more than books and ballet."

Smiling, the dictator got up and stepped to the dais. "I thank you for the welcome. And, you must come to Soviet Union. We will welcome you all in our traditional ways."

Bob Hope was heard to quip, "But what about getting out? Locking people away in their gulags is also a Russian tradition!"

Then Khrushchev turned to Skouras, "My dear brother Greek, I was impressed by your capitalist rags-to-riches story. But I have my own communist rags-to-riches story. I started working as soon as I learned how to walk. I herded cows for the capitalists. That was before I was 15. After that, I worked in a factory for a German. Then I worked in a French-owned mine. Today, I am the premier of the great Soviet state."

Now it was Skouras' turn to heckle. "How many premiers do you have?"

"I will answer that," Khrushchev replied. "I am the premier of the whole country, but there are 15 republics and each has its own premier. Do you have that many?"

"We have two million American presidents of American corporations," Skouras replied.

Unfazed, the premier said, "Mr. Tikhonov, please rise."

At a table in the audience, Nikolai Tikhonov stood up.

"Who is he?" Khrushchev asked. "He is a worker. He became a metallurgical engineer, in charge of huge chemical factories. A third of the ore mined in the Soviet Union comes from his region. Well, Comrade Greek, is that not enough for you?"

"No," Skouras shot back. "That's a monopoly."

"It is a people's monopoly," Khrushchev replied. "He does not possess anything but the pants he wears. It all belongs to the people!"

Earlier, Skouras had mentioned to the audience that American aid helped fight a famine in the Soviet Union in 1922. Now, Khrushchev spoke on the subject and said: Americans sent aid to my country, that is true. But, they also sent an army to crush the Bolshevik revolution. And not only the Americans, but all the capitalist countries of Europe marched upon our country to strangle the new revolution. Never have any of our soldiers been on American soil, but your soldiers were on Russian soil. These are the facts."

"Still," Khrushchev said, "I bear no ill will. Even under those circumstances, we are still grateful for the help you gave."

Khrushchev then recounted his experiences fighting in the Red Army during the Russian civil war. "I was in the Kuban region when we routed the White Guard and threw them into the Black Sea," he said. "I lived in the house of a very interesting bourgeois intellectual family."

"Here I was," Khrushchev went on, "an uneducated miner with coal dust still on my hands, and I and other Bolshevik soldiers, many of them illiterate, were sharing the house with professors and musicians. I remember the landlady asking me: 'Tell me, what do you know about ballet? You're a simple miner, aren't you?' To tell the truth, I didn't know anything about ballet. Not only had I never seen a ballet, I had never seen a ballerina."

The audience laughed.

"I did not know what sort of dish it was or what you ate it with."

That brought more laughter.

"And I said, 'Wait, it will all come. We will have everything—and ballet, too.'"

Khrushchev stopped, looked out at the audience, and said, "Now I have a question for you. Which country has the best ballet? Yours? You do not even have a permanent opera and ballet theater. Your theaters have only what is given to them by rich people. In our country, it is the state that gives the money. And the best ballet is in the Soviet Union. It is our pride."

He rambled on about ballet, named the most famous, about Russian dancers, naming them, then apologized for rambling. After 45 minutes of speaking, he seemed to be approaching an amiable closing. Then he remembered Disneyland.

"Just now, I was told that I could not go to Disneyland," he announced. "I asked, 'Why not? What is it? Do you have rocket-launching pads there?' "

The audience laughed.

"Just listen," he said. "Just listen to what I was told: 'We—which means the American authorities—cannot guarantee your security there.' "

He made a sorrowful face. That got another laugh.

"What is it? Have gangsters taken hold of the place? Your policemen are so tough in your movies. Surely they can restore order if there are any gangsters around. I say, 'I would very much like to see Disneyland.' They say, 'We cannot guarantee your security.' Then what must I do, commit suicide?"

Khrushchev was starting to look more angry than amused. His fist punched the air above his red face.

"That's the situation I find myself in," he said. "For me, such a situation is inconceivable. I cannot find words to explain this to my people."

The audience was baffled. Were they really watching the dictator of the world's largest country throw a temper tantrum because he couldn't go to Disneyland?

Sitting in the audience, Nina Khrushchev told David Niven that she really was disappointed that she couldn't see Disneyland. Hearing that, Sinatra, who was sitting next to Mrs. Khrushchev, leaned over and whispered in Niven's ear. "Screw the cops!" Sinatra said. "Tell the old broad that you and I will take 'em down there this afternoon."

Before long, Khrushchev's tantrum faded away. He grumbled a bit about how he'd been stuffed into a sweltering limousine at the airport instead of a nice, cool convertible. Then he apologized, sort of: "You will say, perhaps, 'What a difficult guest he is.' But I adhere to the Russian rule: 'Eat the bread and salt but always speak your mind.' Please forgive me if I was somewhat hot-headed. But the temperature here contributes to this. Also"—he turned to Skouras —"my Greek friend warmed me up."

Relieved at the change of mood, the audience applauded. Skouras shook Khrushchev's hand and slapped him on the back and the two old, fat, and bald men grinned while the stars, who recognized a good show when they saw one, rewarded them with a standing ovation.

The lunch over, Skouras led his new friend toward the soundstage where *Can-Can* was being filmed, stopping to greet various celebrities along the way. When Skouras spotted Marilyn Monroe in the crowd, he hastened to introduce her to the premier, who'd seen a huge close-up of her face—a clip from *Some Like It Hot*—in a film about American life at an American exhibition in Moscow. Now, Khrushchev shook her hand and looked her over.

"You're a very lovely young lady," he said, smiling.

Later, she would reveal what it was like to be eyeballed by the dictator: "He looked at me the way most men look at me, in a kind of lewd way. And I reacted to his stare by informing him that I was married. 'My husband, Arthur Miller, sends you his greeting' I replied. 'There should be more of this kind of thing. It would help both our countries understand each other.' "

Skouras led Khrushchev and his family across the street to Sound Stage 8 and up a rickety wooden staircase to a box above the stage. Sinatra appeared onstage wearing a turn-of-the-century French suit, his costume. He played a French lawyer who falls in love with a dancer, played by Shirley MacLaine, who was arrested for performing a banned dance called the can-can. "This is a movie about a lot of pretty girls and the fellows who like pretty girls," Sinatra announced.

Khrushchev grinned and applauded.

"Later in this picture, we go to a saloon," Sinatra continued. "A saloon is a place where you go to drink."

Khrushchev laughed at that, too. He seemed to be having a good time.

Shooting commenced; lines were delivered, and after a dance number that left no doubts why the cancan had once been banned, many spectators—American and Russian—wondered: *Why did they choose this for Khrushchev?*

"It was the worst choice imaginable," one diplomat later recalled. "When a male dancer dived under Shirley MacLaine's skirt and emerged holding what seemed to be her red panties, the Americans in the audience gave an audible gasp of dismay, while the Russians sat in stolid, disapproving silence."

Later, Khrushchev would denounce the dance as pornographic exploitation, though at the time he seemed happy enough.

"I was watching him," said Lodge, "and he seemed to be enjoying it."

Sasha, Khrushchev's son-in-law, didn't know what to think about the scene and movie at the time. And later when the premier asked him, '*What does this mean?*' he recalled saying 'It might be political provocation, or nothing more than American stupidity.'

Whether Khrushchev liked it was questionable; but what was certain was that his wife Nina did not like it. Though Gary Cooper relayed the offer to take her to Disneyland, she told him that she could no longer do that. And she added, "I hope the Indians win next time."

Did Nina also tell her husband that, and was the Cuban missile crisis the result? Sasha believes so.

THE FINAL RESOLVE
OF A REVOLUTIONARY

*Che Guevara once said that truth
is not important, nor is friendship,
love, or life, only the final end.*

The message arrived late on October 8, Bishop's 50th birthday. It was hand-carried by the FBI Agent in Charge in Miami and read: "CG has been caught and will speak to no one but you. You have 24 hours to save him and avoid disclosure. There will be a plane standing by at the airport. WWR to send written instructions."

Bishop was expecting this, having read about Che Guevara's capture by Bolivian forces in the papers. He'd been out of the CIA by almost three years now, three very lucrative years after starting his own geopolitical intelligence service, and issuing analysis weekly in a publication called *The Insight* on "breaking news" events around the world at $1,500 per issue. His subscribers included Fortune 500 companies, universities other intelligence professionals, and international government agencies. Was Bolivia among them, he wondered? What leverage could he use on them?

After flying non-stop for 10 hours, and undergoing aerial refueling, the unmarked Learjet landed at Vallegrande, Bolivia. Bishop was met by the CIA Station Chief and the Deputy Ambassador, both of whom were overweight and out of breath after walking only 20 yards from their station wagon. Bishop bounded down the small steps and a short way to greet them and also felt a little out of breath and light-headed.

"What the hell's the elevation here?" Bishop asked.

"It's close to eight thousand feet, and it'll feel a lot worse when we get to where we're going, which is another two thousand feet higher," the CIA guy Martin said.

"I always thought you'd make it to the top, Martin, but this is ridiculous," said Bishop.

"And everyone knew you'd make it to the stars, and I'll be damned if you did, Mr. Ambrose Davis Bishop, in person! Harvard Class of 1940, All-American, Ace fighter pilot, Yale Law, CIA from the beginning, and now intelligence briefer to the world!"

Ignored was Andrews, the Deputy Ambassador. "We need to get going," he abruptly said. "We still got another couple of hours to go." He said that as officious as he could under the circumstances.

Bishop looked around at the bleak landscape. Who the hell wants to retire here, he thought, only a guy who wants to avoid getting caught, by both sides.

The road was asphalt only into the small town. After they circled the plaza and headed north it became a dirt road replete with potholes, large ruts, and runoff streams. Bishop thought he'd get some sleep after he got off the jet —since he'd never been able to sleep on planes, but that seemed impossible on the drive as well.

"Oh, I have a cable for you, from National Security Advisor Rostow," said Andrews.

"You've read it, no doubt. So, what's it say?" Said Bishop.

Andrew looked peeved. "Yes, I have, since I am cleared for it."

Bishop said nothing but stared Andrews down.

"It is my shop, after all." Said Andrews.

"For the moment," said Bishop. "And it's also your shit I have to clean up."

"The new Chief of Police for La Higuera was informed about… The arrangement," said Martin.

"Was he? Not well enough, obviously," Bishop said, smacking the door to his side. "And are you going to give me the cable? Or are you going to forget about that too?"

"I didn't forget about the arrangement… You can't blame me for that!"

Andrews drew an envelope from his breast pocket and threw it at Bishop.

Bishop took the envelop, and without opening it, slowly tore it into small pieces. Then he threw the pieces at Andrew. "I know what it says —there could only be one thing it could say."

Bishop leaned back and closed his eyes. "How's he holding up," he said with a yawn.

Martin spoke: "Che took two shots, one to his left thigh and another to his right arm. Both bullets went clean through, but he lost a lot of blood. He's weak —and really pissed, but otherwise OK."

"Wake me when we get there," said Bishop.

The first time Bishop met Che Guevara was in 1955. Bishop represented himself as the relief coordinator for a Christian charity, though it didn't take long before Che realized who he really was — a senior field operator for the CIA whose assignment was to turn one of Fidel Castro's top lieutenants into a CIA asset. He did that, several times in fact, and was turned back several times as well, by Castro, and by Dashkov, his opposite number from the KGB.

Bishop was brainy and street smart, fluent in Spanish and Russian, handsome and bi-sexual, and Harvard-educated where he got to know JFK. Later he was the president's personal choice to be the back-channel to both Khrushchev and Castro during the Cuban Missile Crisis.

But Bishop was also brash and disrespectful to those who he considered less intelligent and informed than he —which included virtually everyone he met in Washington. He left the CIA after JFK's assassination, after which his style of irreverent service branded him a pariah.

In Spanish, the Chief of Police said: "This is not the United States and you are not in charge —I am. I have complete authority here, and not you, or anyone else is going to order me to release him. Do you understand?" The Chief was having his desayuno at his desk and sat concentrating on his food, slowly eating his huevos con chorizo, and not making eye contact with the three men that entered minutes before.

Andrews looked flustered. "Just call your President, that's all I'm asking you to do… Only that."

"Why? I am the law here. There is no judge to decide these things. I do. The three were drunk and killed two men, including my brother-in-law, two nights ago at a wedding celebration. I decided that they will be executed for what they did. And they will be tomorrow, at sunrise."

"May we question them?" Said Bishop.

"They have already been questioned… That is enough.."

Bishop took off a signet ring made of gold with a small diamond in the center and placed in on the desk. In Spanish, he said: "For ten minutes with the one with the beard."

The Police Chief looked up and met Bishop's gaze. "Five minutes, no more. And I must be present."

"Two minutes, and no one else in the room," Bishop said.

Bishop opened the door. It was a small room, no more than eight by eight feet. There were two buckets near the door, a small stool in one corner with a candle on it, and a mat in the other corner with Che on top of it. Propped up, and barely recognizable, he was very thin and frail, and wheezed from his asthma. His dark hair was very curly and long, reaching to his shoulders, and his beard was twice the size it was when he last saw him in 1963.

"Still alive, I see," said Bishop. "I thought you would be dead by now."

"I'm happy to see you too, *cabron*," said Che.

Bishop smiled. He had formed a bond with Che many years ago, and that still continued despite the passage of time. They both shared many of the same attributes. Both were well educated and savvy in more earthy ways, good looking, and had reached lofty positions despite not giving a fuck about it. Better get on with it though, Bishop thought, we have only minutes to talk.

"I need to know," Bishop said. "Is the deal still on? The removal of Kennedy and Khrushchev went right on schedule. Are the next two still in place?

"No," said Che, "It never was 'on.' "

"What? But, we did our part, and your side did yours…"

"Castro never agreed to it. Any of it. That was all my doing," said Che. "I forged his signature, as I did virtually everything else I passed you."

There was silence.

"It was necessary to do something or else the whole world would be at war… Nuclear war. And Cuba would be the center of it. Havana would be gone like Hiroshima or Nagasaki. And, of course, next would come DC, Moscow and—" Che stopped. "You doubt that?"

Bishop was leaning against the door, stunned.

"Does anyone else know this?" Said Bishop.

"I never told anyone, except you, now."

"Good." Bishop wanted to tell Che that he had always suspected that something never seemed right about the plan by the intelligence services of both sides to intervene in what their bosses were doing in bringing the world close to nuclear war, but to have it acknowledged still came as a surprise to him. And that he, Bishop, the ultimate spy, hadn't guessed who was behind it, rattled him. It was Che, on his own —the Marxist revolutionary, "the butcher of La Cabaña" and other mass murders— had saved the world. Ironic that those images of Che on T-shirts have it right, he is a hero, but for the wrong reasons.

"Well, I guess it's time to say *adios, mi amigo,*" said Bishop.

"You are going to see to it that I am removed, aren't you?" Said Che.

"Of course," said Bishop. "In minutes."

Bishop closed the door and sighed. He thought back to what Che had written to his father after dropping out of medical school, and joining Castro's July 26 movement as a guerrilla. "The final resolve of a revolutionary is to die for the great justice of the people's cause."

He looked at the Chief of Police who was standing near the door and gave a slight wave of his hand as if to say, I'm done. And then he took off his gold wedding band, handed it to the Chief, and said, "*Ahora… Now.*"

The Chief of Police accepted the ring and signaled to two uniformed men with rifles to go into the room.

As Bishop walked down the hall to meet with Andrews and Martin again, breathing deeply the rarefied air, he had taken only a few steps before he heard the two shots.

DEATH, THE DESTROYER OF WORLDS

An interview with J. Robert Oppenheimer, "the father" of the nuclear age, sealed until now.

When J. Robert Oppenheimer witnessed the first detonation of an atomic bomb on July 16, 1945, he uttered the words: "Now I am become Death, the destroyer of worlds". It was, according to what he told others present there, a piece of Hindu scripture from the Bhagavad-Gita; he said he had turned to Hinduism and was a follower.

Appointed as wartime director of the Los Alamos project that developed the atom bomb, Oppenheimer has been called "the father" of the nuclear age. It brought to a swift end World War Two, after which, almost as quick, he led a group of scientists that sought to end the use of atomic weapons for war. Yet, he lied when he said he was non-partisan on political matters and had never even voted. He was a registered Communist Party member and had even held meetings with local party members in his home.

More questionable was that he may have helped Soviet spies gain atomic secrets which led to the Soviet Union acquiring atomic weapons as well. That was the basis of the government's decision to strip him of his security clearance, and that led to his retirement, at age 49 to a small ranch in New Mexico.

That was essentially all I knew about Oppenheimer when in 1961, I was charged with learning all I could about him in order to advise President John F. Kennedy on whether to award him The Medal of Freedom, the country's highest civilian honor.

Working on a tight deadline of six weeks, I researched his life, tracing the convoluted path that led to his appointment, at age 37, to head the group of scientists charged with developing the first nuclear weapons; and I interviewed over two dozen of his colleagues and acquaintances before speaking with him personally.

My meeting with Oppenheimer is memorialized below. Note that it reflects my observations and feelings at the time, as well as my questions and his answers. My formal opinion to JFK on the question of whether he should receive the honor was prepared later. This was for my own use, and has been sealed until now.

The one thing that there is no question about is the brilliance of Oppenheimer. His achievements in physics are legendary, and according to some, on par with De Vinci, Newton, and even Einstein. And they include so many that he could have been awarded the Nobel Prize numerous times over, and yet wasn't for seemingly political reasons —his association with the atomic bomb. For many in the scientific community, he symbolized the errant thinking of some researchers that their work could be controlled and not be used for malevolent purposes. And that moral dilemmas in the nuclear world were theirs to resolve, and not relegated to lesser minds.

We met at the offices of Oppenheimer's lawyer in Taos, New Mexico, in what appeared to be a utility room, small and ugly, that housed a copy machine and supplies, as well as a small table and two chairs. By design? The reflection of how he felt about this meeting?

He walked in late by twenty minutes, didn't greet me or say a word, just nodded in my direction after putting down his smoking paraphernalia on the table and clearing his throat. I felt like a student in one of his classes back when he was a Professor of Physics at Princeton; and I sensed that he viewed me as a member of a firing squad at his execution.

Me: I am recording this, as per agreement with your lawyer, and will make a copy for your use as well. [A nod of approval from JRO.] And I have to emphasis once again that I am not an academic, I have no credentials in the physical sciences, nor know anything about nuclear physics, except maybe what I have read in magazines about you and your work.

JRO: Understood.

Me: You lost your security clearance exactly nine years ago tomorrow, on April 1, 1954.

JRO: Yes, on April Fools Day, but who was the fool? They, the board members of the Atomic Energy Commission, who, by the way, also lacked credentials as scientists, or I, who accepted their findings and did not appeal the decision. Many said I should appeal, but others said it wasn't worth it."

Me: Who counseled you to appeal… Or, more important, who said you shouldn't and why?

JRO: Fermi, Lawrence, Compton… All the top nuclear physicists' had quit by then. Even Einstein told me a plumbers' license is more valuable and practical now.

Me: A plumber didn't win the war by dropping an atom bomb on Japan.

JRO: I didn't have anything to do with that... dropping the bomb on Japan, that is, which was a political decision, and was wrong. I only helped develop, along with thousands of others, basic research on nuclear fission.

Me: The Manhattan Project, which was intended to deliver to the military the capability of a super weapon, took almost four years, employed almost half a million people, and cost over two billion dollars; and you believe that was only a research project? That the atomic bomb you built should not have been used to end World War Two?

JRO: Correct. [He seemed to expect the question, and answered it quickly, without hesitation. Then, after additional thought, continued.] We made it in order to prevent it being used against us... Not by us.

Me: To prevent it being used by Hitler?

JRO: Yes, but we later learned there wasn't any German atomic bomb project, only a plan for one... But then we used it all the same, against the Japanese.

Me: But weren't you asked at some point if it should be used against Japan?

[At this point, he got up, stretched, looked over in my direction, but seemingly saw through me into memories. He turned toward the small window, and, peering out, continued.]

JRO: We weren't asked *whether* it should be used, but only *how* it should be used in order to produce the maximum effect.

Me: But weren't you privy to a letter from physicist Franck and others that recommended a public demonstration of the bomb over a desert instead of its use on Japan?

[He looked at me with hostility and almost outright anger. In order to get beyond those feelings, I took out a copy of the letter I referenced and placed it on the table. He didn't acknowledge or even glance at it.]

JRO: I was in no position to decide the issue, nor even officially asked. Nevertheless, a few of us had our arguments, for and against.

Me: Which side were you on?

[Again, he looked out the window before answering.]

JRO: Most were against… And that was my leaning, though I was undecided. I thought it might just come off as a firecracker, and that might have been worse, and prolong the war.

Me: Did that not mean that you were *for* its military use and *for* dropping it on Japan without warning?

[He looked at me and leaned forward, as if he was about to pounce, as a lion or tiger might.]

JRO: It most certainly did not mean that. No. We were physicists — not the military, not politicians, and definitely *not* in charge. [He stopped, looked up at the ceiling, and then towards the window again; and continued speaking.] That was the time of very heavy fighting in Okinawa, the fieriest of struggles there, and many deaths, in the thousands, on both sides. It was a horrible decision, in many respects, but made by others.

Me: Didn't you write the official report on the effects of the bomb on Hiroshima?

JRO: It was written by others over my signature, yes; according to information and data supplied by others as well.

Me: And did you not state there that the dropping of the bomb had been a good thing, and very successful?

[He breathed heavily, and said, almost in a whisper:]

JRO: Yes, that it was technically successful, and it was.

Me: Only technically? It ended the war, didn't it?

[With full voice again and vigor:]

JRO: It ended one war, and started another. And we have been on the brink of nuclear annihilation ever since. That was what we created… What we committed as sin.

Me: You consider creation of what you did a commission of sin?

JRO: I guess we don't mean the same thing.

Me: You devoted yourself with such single-mindedness to to your tasks, with hundred-per-cent loyalty, to the atomic bomb —

JRO: —Correction, we always referred to it as "the devise."—

Me: —and later, with the hydrogen bomb, you adopted an entirely different attitude, against that weapon.

JRO: It doesn't bear comparison, I think.

Me: And why not?

JRP: The target was too small… We were told that the atom bomb was the only means of bringing the war to an end quickly and successfully.

Me: You don't have to defend the dropping of the bomb to me, Mr. Oppenheimer, I was a high school senior at the time, and was very glad the war came to an end when it did.

JRO: Yes, the war came to an end, but it was also the means by which hundreds of thousands of men, women and children came to… *an end*.

[At that point he sat, put his hands out to look at them. They were shaking.]

JRO: I read, in the New York Times, that if America hadn't won the war I would have been tried as a war criminal by the Japanese.

Me: You read that in the New York Times?

JRO: Yes… In the Letters to the Editor section.

Me: Who reads that?

JRO: I do!

[He goes to the window and peers out, seemingly a thousand miles away.]

Me: Your associations with scientific research concerning nuclear fission ended with your security clearance being revoked by the Atomic Energy Committee, a body you helped establish. In your opinion, was that decision not justified?

JRO: Not at all.

Me: The basis of their decision included your actions and associations with known communists…

JRO: …All known before I was appointed to head the Los Alamos group, and stemming from activities dating back to the 1930's. The army knew that, as well as the FBI. The only new allegation was that I was opposed to the development of the hydrogen bomb.

Me: And were you?

JRO: Yes, on moral and other grounds; and that I turned other scientists against the hydrogen bomb, that I considerably slowed down the development of the hydrogen bomb.

Me: In your opinion, was that allegation not justified?

JRO: It is not true.

Me: Not true in any respect?

JRO: In no respect at all. Ever since the development of weapons of war from atomic research two world powers have been facing each other like scorpions in a bottle, each with raised lethal stingers —millimeters from the other; with blame placed on the birth mothers of the scorpions, as it were, and not the people who placed the scorpions in the bottle. And those same people are trying to persuade America that the blame lies with traitors.

Me: I have the transcript here of your testimony before the Atomic Energy Commission. Is there anything you wish to alter or correct in your prior statements?

JRO: Yes, that the quote attributed to me at the time of the Trinity test in 1945 be corrected. I should have connected it to the Hydrogen bomb, for it is *death, the destroyer of worlds!*

Me: Let me read from your testimony before the Atomic Energy Commission. You said there, and I quote, "My duty was always as a consultant, to advise, and not to decide." Yet later you also said this: "Without my participation, the development of atomic weapons would not have been possible, in the manner and way that they were achieved. I was indispensable, I was the one who made them happen." How does that square with your position that you were only a consultant?

[He looked like he'd been hit in the head after that bare, blunt question. He opened his mouth to speak and nothing came out. His eyes glazed, his face lost all its color and his entire body slackened, as if all life had exited from it.]

Me: Mr. Oppenheimer, are you OK? Can you continue?

[No apparent change. I don't even think he heard me.]

Me: We can take a ten minute break, if you'd like?

[His eyes blink several times and some color returns to his face.]

Me: Mr Oppenheimer, I believe you are an extraordinary individual, a very complicated man, a man that takes a great deal of knowing, a man beyond measure in gifts and accomplishments. And like all gifted men, unique, sole, not conventional, not quite anybody else that ever was or will be. Does this mean that we should apply different standards of morality? I think not.

Some men are simple, and their acts equally simple. That doesn't mean that the standards are any different for them. They bear the same examination of what they are, of what they stand for, how they act, and what they do and accomplish. And what they mean to the country.

You have to answer the direct, honest, and, yes, ugly question of whether you were responsible for every death in Nagasaki, Hiroshima, and every death associated with nuclear power, from the blast at Trinity on. In that respect, you served the interests of the United States of America, which we all love and want to protect, but further, bear the consequences of your actions on its behalf. That's not only fair, but honorable. And patriotic. And principled.

[He is sitting upright once again, and almost as composed as before.]

JRO: Thank you. And I'd like to correct the record once again. Previously I sought to strike my statement connecting the atomic bomb to the Hindu scripture and applying it to the Hydrogen bomb. Now I know how I meant it then, and now.

It is I who is death, the destroyer of worlds!

PUTIN AND THE
NOBEL PRIZE

This story is highly speculative and is based on conjecture, surmise and inference, not on established facts.

"Someone is getting rich from my books, and I wish to stop it." That was Tom's introduction to the case that sent him to Moscow in December of 1998, and which almost got him killed. He was having dinner with his wife on a cruise ship with dinner companions he had just met. They were Russian, as is his wife, Tanya, and she met them at the pool that afternoon. They were Muscovites, urban and sophisticated as they come. They were seemingly drawn to Tanya because she was the first Russian they'd met after almost a month away from home.

After the usual introductions of names, where each was from, about children, grandchildren, and even great-grandchildren on the part of the couple from Moscow, they later got into what each did for a living. The usual small talk on such an occasion. The Russian couple, as it turned out, were world-class scientists, on a round-the-world cruise funded in part by money from the Nobel Prize she had won some years before. On Tom's part, he was newly retired from law, and this was his first extended vacation he had ever had. It wasn't a world cruise for his wife and him, only a leg of it from Istanbul to London, three weeks, plus several days at both ends.

You are a lawyer? Natalia Bakitsa's eyes lit up when she learned that. The next sentence that followed was, "Someone is getting rich from my books, and I wish to stop it." It seems her books, almost two dozen of them which were required reading during Soviet times, were now showing up in colleges all around the world. Someone was translating them and selling copies, all without permission, crediting her or paying her royalties. She was used to the lack of royalties under the former Soviet Union, but at least they acknowledged her as the author. Now, post-glasnost, and under new laws of the Russian Federation, she was being denied both recognition and payment for her work.

Natalia and Alek Bakitsa weren't exactly penniless before Natalia won the Nobel Prize. They were a power couple of the highest order in Russia, as they had been under the former Soviet Union where academic status towered above everything else and translated to privilege and the best available in the Soviet system. She was wearing designer clothes and enough jewelry to stock a glass case at Tiffany's, while he projected status in the latest Italian blazer cut lean and tight.

To say that Natalia was interested in getting paid for her work product was an understatement —she was obsessed with it. And the dinner conversation that night seldom went beyond it, except for the usual detour when his last name was given, Darrow.

"Are you related to the famous lawyer, Clarence Darrow?" Natalia asked.

Tom got this all the time from Americans, and now a Russian couple, on the high seas off Malta? *Why not, it's a small world,* thought Tom.

"Clarence Darrow was my grandfather."

"Outstanding linage for a lawyer."

"The best."

Natalia's detour ended with that. "What do you know about international copyright laws?" She asked.

"Not a damn thing," Tom responded.

Unfazed, she replied, "It's never too late to learn." And then she went on to give him the details of her situation, something she'd probably said numerous times to numerous people: Her books were being published in places that had no copyright protection, countries such as San Marino, Somalia, and Turkmenistan. Printing and marketing was done outside those countries in the usual places, Paris, London and New York, but with smaller printing houses. She had retained a lawyer in Paris about this "theft of intellectual property," but he had been unsuccessful stopping it after almost five years on the case, and had burned through a retainer and additional monies that exceeded almost a quarter of a million dollars.

"*Almost a quarter million?*" Tom repeated when she said that, taken aback. "How much are the rights worth?"

"A reasonable estimate, according to a forensic accountant, would be $20 million, and that was almost three years ago."

"That would make you a rich woman."

"I am a rich woman. That would make me a *very* rich woman. More important, it would give me the recognition and credit that I deserve."

"That it would," Tom said, with some appreciation for her purpose finally.

"And something else," she said. "Something your grandfather

would understand… Justice."

"Where is the venue now?" He asked.

"Paris, for the most part, but he's filed in numerous other places, always unsuccessful."

"Your lawyer's a Parisian, of course, he would. What you have to do is go to where you'll have a friendly court, to Moscow, to get your 'justice' finally. A judgment there would be binding on every major distributor in the world."

"Yes! And you will do that for me!" Her eyes were lit, on fire really, as she savored victory somehow from what Tom said.

"Natalia, I didn't mean to encourage you or mislead you in any way about what I could do for you. I can't take your case because I don't know anything about copyright law. I'm also retired. And I have a wife who wants to travel finally after so many years…"

Just then, Tom's wife, Tanya, spoke, "Don't make me the reason why you won't take this case. Things were stolen from me too after I left Russia. And I have always wanted justice."

Tom knew then he was licked. After dinner, he picked up Natalia's file on her litigation from her cabin. And the next day, Tom called his old firm and asked them to set him up again in his old office, transfer his former paralegal and secretary from other assignments, and to put him back on the payroll as of the previous night with three hours of case billings on the Bakitsa case. He was back.

◆ ◆ ◆

Bill Clinton was having the worst year of his presidency in 1998. The scandal involving Monica Lewinsky dominated the news through the summer of that year, followed by the very damning findings of the Independent Counsel investigation released in September that Clinton had committed perjury and obstruction of justice. That led to the House of Representatives voting for his impeachment in December.

Foreign affairs were not high on the president's agenda that year. There was the Good Friday peace accords signed by the parties to end the long conflict in Northern Ireland, which Clinton helped conclude, but virtually nothing else of any consequence. Clinton sent missiles targeting Al Qaeda training camps in retaliation for bombing of US embassies in Kenya and Tanzania, but those were seen by the press as attempts to distract from the Lewinsky revelations and the Independent Counsel investigation. That's why Ambrose Bishop was summoned in by the president, to take care of something so that it wouldn't prove embarrassing to Clinton.

Clinton had met with Bishop once before, right after he came into office, when Bishop filled him in on a CIA operation that was "off the books," a plot to assassinate Boris Yeltsin by a group of young Russian oligarchs. They were upset by attempts to destroy or curtail them, and planned to replace him with one of their own. That plot failed, but there was a new one afoot, and this time the oligarchs were trying to do the opposite, stave off the Communist leader's killing by those who wanted him replaced with an upstart, an ex-KGB named Vladimir Putin.

Bishop, who was Putin's opposite number when both were in East Germany in the late Eighties, was the perfect operative for that. They were on different sides, but routinely socialized while viewing first hand the fall of the Berlin Wall, and later the collapse of the Communist East German government. Both were reassigned in 1990; Putin to Saint Petersburg and then to Moscow on a fast track to KGB leadership, and Bishop as head of CIA's covert operations. Yet they kept in secret and unshared touch with each other.

When Clinton learned from the CIA of the current plot, he had to ponder the agonizing question of whether it was America's business to become involved in the internal affairs of Russia, but first decide whether Putin would be a good replacement —good for the U.S., that is. As Carter learned earlier in Iran, regime change is not always good, no matter the sentiment of the populace.

Yeltsin had been an improvement over most of his predecessors, yet he was in poor health, intoxicated most of the time, and likely would be replaced soon anyway. Sergey Kiriyenko was seen as Yeltsin's nominal successor as Prime Minister. Was Putin preferred over Kiriyenko?

Clinton sat on the intelligence for some time, but decided that even it might be leaked at some point. What to do about it? In Washington, Clinton learned, you can put off decisions by studying them further. He would dispatch Bishop to learn all he could about the plot and take the measure of Putin. Ultimately, Clinton was going to have to decide who's side to be on, Yeltsin or Putin?

This was not Bishop's first visit to the Oval Office. His first was in JFK's time, and numerous others followed, in the administrations of Johnson, Nixon, Ford, Carter, and Reagan. They were usually private meetings and always concerned the most confidential of matters. And Clinton followed the precedent of others in that conversations were not recorded, and direct orders were orally given by the president. Betraying nationals who wanted to overturn their government in places such as Chile, Brazil, Guatemala, Iran, Vietnam, and even Russia was not new, but at least keeping it from becoming publicly known could be.

"Mr. President, good to see you again," said Bishop when he was finally ushered in the side door to the Oval Office, almost an hour after he and Clinton were scheduled to meet.

"Good to see you too," said Clinton from behind his desk. The president remained sitting and nodded with a friendly smile, pointing to the chair alongside.

Clinton got right to the point. "Remember that business of 1994, the threat against Yeltsin?"

"Yes, of course. All the loose ends were cleaned up, as I recall."

"They were indeed, thanks to you. But now *we think* there's another 'business' of the same sort —so I'm told. And I need you to find out what it's all about. Solid facts, from the best sources, — first hand, if possible. And what I should do about it."

"Same rules apply?"

"Yes, of course. But there's one wrinkle to it. The plotters may include Putin, and he may be the one to come out on top. Is that a problem for you?"

Bishop's gaze didn't change. "That makes it complicated, of course, but not an obstacle to what I have to do."

Clinton looked down at his desk, took a deep breath, and then said, "Just bear this in mind: Do whatever you can to protect Yeltsin. They have a democracy there now, and we should care about that these days."

"I will, I assure you of that, Mr. President."

"Take care, and best of luck!"

"I will do that, sir, and best of luck to you."

Bishop hesitated and then added, "You know that most of the occupants of this office did much worse, some *far worse*, and never paid the price for it.

Clinton winked and leaned back in his chair. Then he broke into a smile and said, "Some of the stories I hear from the Secret Service... I couldn't imagine them happening here." He paused, and his eyes went to the painting of George Washington. "And the first President, George —I can't tell a lie— Washington, witnessed it all!"

Bishop's meeting shortly after that with CIA Director George Tenet went less amicably. Their contacts had always been detached and distant, partly because Tenet wanted it that way, for accountability purposes. The less he knew about covert operations, the better. Tenet was never told about the earlier plot against Yeltsin, and Bishop didn't brief him on the latest. He only told Tenet he was going away on a confidential mission for the President.

"Need any assets?" Tenet asked.

"Nothing unusual," Bishop said. "I'll take my usual draw from accounting here, and I need a 'heads up' to accounting there at the embassy in Moscow for additional funds. Oh, and a young operative, Bill Deutch, to serve as my "son" there again. He speaks Russian with a Ukrainian accent and would be perfect for my cover story that we're there at KGB headquarters to track down relatives that may have been "detained" years ago by the KGB."

"You want to go into the Lubyanya?" Tenet seemed genuinely surprised. "Half the Russians that went in ended up in the Gulags, and they were the lucky ones. The other half were cremated there, after being tortured to death."

"That was before *perestroik*a and *glasnost*, not now. They've changed their ways, or haven't you heard? Gorbachev announced that himself." Said Bishop with a wry smile.

"Gorbachev's no longer in charge, or haven't you heard that?" Tenet snipped back.

"Rest assured, George, I read all the news clippings you political appointees share with us, no matter how dated or wrong they are. Anyway, I need to get into the Lubyanya. That's necessary to get even close to Putin now… *Especially now.*"

Bishop thought he'd drop that remark on Tenet just to irritate him, and it worked.

"I don't want to know a fuckin' thing about why you're going there. And if you mention anything more, I'll personally leak what you say and blow your assignment. Then you can explain to the President why you can't do what he asked."

Bishop only turned and smiled. *That* mission was accomplished.

"Tom, you'll need a Sherpa to guide you up that legal procedural mountain in Moscow, and dress warmly because you'll face the harshest, coldest, most bone-chilling environment there in the courts, let alone outside. Goodness knows I tried, and I know Russian," said Sy Kirov. Someone referred him to Tom as a Russian law expert.

"And there are few lawyers there in Moscow who will partner with you regardless of how much you pay them," said Sy. "They get ostracized for doing that and lose clients. Some do it, but they're too green, or too burned out that they wouldn't be helpful to you anyway."

Tom checked the lawyer referral book in the law library. Moscow had only five lawyers listed with copyright law as one of their specialties. He called them all and selected one based on their English-speaking skills. He didn't want *that* headache as well.

What Tom had learned from Sy and others who had handled legal matters in Russia was that getting a judgment in an *arbitrazh* court, the civil court equivalent in Russia, was a towering achievement, but not as difficult as enforcement and collecting anything on it.

"Waste of time" was what he was told —literally a hundred-to-one chance of it, according to a Swedish lawyer who practiced there for a few years. That was during the 1990s when debt-related cases increased dramatically during the turbulent times after the Soviet Union collapsed.

"Self-help using Russian Mafia-type enforcers was the only way to go," the Swedish lawyer told him. "That or knowing someone in the KGB or high up in the party —preferably both."

With all that going against him, Tom thought himself quite lucky to have met someone who seemed "connected" in Moscow. They met at the First Class lounge of Aeroflot at National Airport before boarding the flight to Moscow. The flight was delayed for three hours and Tom got to know the man quite well.

He was Tom's age, and a retiree like himself who was going there to try to learn about a relative who had "disappeared" while being detained by the KGB. The man's name was Windsor, and he was quite fit for his age. He was taller than Tom, had dark blond hair with some gray, and almost movie-star handsome. And he had a precise way of talking as if each word he spoke was to be etched in stone.

"Mind if I go with you when you make the rounds at the Lubyanya?" Tom asked Windsor.

"Not if you don't mind waiting needless hours or even days there getting the run-around from one KGB bureaucrat to another," said Windsor. "And, I'm going to make a pest of myself… With the possibility that pest control measures there may be dangerous."

"With two of us doing that, their go-to fumigation methods may not be employed," said Tom.

◆ ◆ ◆

"Shit!" was what Bill Deutch said, followed by "Fuck, piss!" In disappointment, when he heard he wouldn't get to serve as Bishop's "son" again, as he had years earlier. He had been in on the prior plot against Yeltsin, his first covert operation since he joined CIA. And what an assignment! Working with a legend on probably the most important operation of its kind ever. Since then, though, he'd been working at the Moscow embassy as a Public Affairs officer just waiting for another like assignment, though he figured he'd already completed his once-in-a-career mission.

Bill kept busy in his cover as a member of the U.S. diplomatic delegation by reading all daily publications in Moscow, given his native fluency in Russian, and it paid off. Almost half of the items originating from the Moscow embassy forwarded to Washington were from Deutch. In bold caps, one day was mention of an attorney, Tom Darrow, who was coming to Moscow, retained by Nobel Prize-winning Natalia Bakitsa to pursue litigation on her behalf for copyright infringement.

Bakistsa was an enigma to the CIA because she was the first Russian Nobel Prize winner who was heralded in Pravda, the official government newspaper of the Communist Party. Previous winners such as Boris Pasternak and Aleksandr Solzhenitsyn had not been accorded that: the Kremlin had forced Pasternak to reject his Nobel Prize; Solzhenitsyn had declined to travel to Stockholm to collect his prize, for fear he would not be allowed to return.

Worse still was Andrei Sakharov. Regarded by some as Russia's greatest scientist and principle designer of the Soviet hydrogen bomb. He was not allowed to travel to Oslo to receive his Nobel Peace prize, awarded him for his activism against nuclear weapons, and instead was sent to "internal exile" in Gorky.

Maybe the Kremlin didn't want to pick another fight with the Nobel Prize committee, the CIA reasoned. Or, and this was the theory of some, she had some friends high up in the party or the KGB.

The item on Bakistsa found by Deutch was included in the CIA Daily Briefing prepared for the President, and read by Bishop, who changed his travel plans soon after. Windsor would be a good name to use since it was the name the Royal Family in England adopted in 1917, partly in response to the Russian attempts to overthrow and assassinate Czar Nicholas II.

Natalia Bakista was named Natalia Uziev after her birth in 1925, in the Chadinov District of Leningrad. She was the only child of gifted musicians who performed with the Leningrad symphony. Even in the worst days after the Russian Revolution, the suffering during the world-wide depression, and the fighting and starvation during World War Two, her home was an enclave from most miseries.

The family had to put up with inconsistent supplies of water, food, and clothing, but less so than most others. They had special privileges because of their talents. Natalia inherited their musical talents, but also a superior analytical mind that was obvious in math and science. And the family were all Communist Party members, not nominal as some were, but robust advocates for the party.

One of the saddest days in the Uziev household was the day Josef Stalin died. Her father praised him almost every day that Natalia recalled, and openly cried —the first time she ever saw him cry— when he died. And when Nikita Khrushchev succeeded him, her father gave up his musical career to serve in party positions as a propagandist, and spent the rest of his days defending the party and its positions, first in Leningrad, and then in Moscow.

Natalia was granted a medical degree at age 20, one of the first women and youngest to achieve that because of the Soviet Union's need for doctors during World War Two, graduating at the top of her class. Her newly acquired skills were put to the test treating thousands of injured soldiers even though she began to practice at the university hospital weeks after the war officially ended on May 8, 1945.

Moving from the dorm to a private apartment she shared with two other women was a major step in Natalia's life. One became a lover, and the other her mentor. The latter was Jelena, an economist with a gift for languages who taught Natalia more than a dozen of them; and the former, Tatianna, a botanist who made all of life meaningful to her.

Natalia was with the two women for only three years before she married Alek Bakitsa, a physicist who taught at the university because that's what women were expected to do for the state: be productive in work and procreate at least three children as well. Natalia had five children, even overachieving on that.

Though Natalia had come from favored family connections, she was no match for Alek on that. His father was a general staff officer at the outbreak of World War II, and later one of the heroes of the Battle of Kursk. He headed the Soviet forces which stopped, for the first time in the war, a frontal attack by the Germans. Though killed in the fighting, he was given credit for turning the German attack into a retreat after only a week. In the Soviet hierarchy of heroes of the state, there was no higher tier than that.

Natalia used her connections and her raw native intelligence to first return to university and take advanced degrees in physics and chemistry, and then was given her own research lab, free to conduct pure research that she thought essential and not what the state required. Soon she was joined by others, almost as talented, and her lab became a place where breakthroughs in science occurred with regularity. It became the leading research institute in the Soviet Union, where three Nobel Prize winners achieved their greatest success.

That was why the CIA tried to lure Natalia to defect and continue her work in the West, and why the KGB used everything in its arsenal to not let that happen. At the center of that conflict were Putin and Bishop, with Putin and the KGB prevailing… At least initially, according to Bishop.

◆ ◆ ◆

Boris Yeltsin was having the worst year of his presidency in 1998. Unlike his counterpart in the U.S., his problems were not about sexual dalliances or other personal scandals, but something more meaningful to the Russian psyche… Russia's preeminence and influence in the world. First, there was the disastrous state of the Russian economy. Though Russia had always been poor, there was a sense that it was a force to be reckoned with in international affairs. Under Yeltsin, however, Russia had become even poorer and also held in contempt in international affairs.

Afghanistan was a disaster, of course. So too were the attempts to keep Chechnya in line. Weekly, if not daily terrorist attacks in Moscow were the result. Most Kremlin insiders, though, saw Yeltsin's performance during the Kosovo War as the final straw. All of Yeltsin's wishes and aspirations there were disregarded. The Russian views simply didn't matter to the West. Even Yeltsin's only triumph there turned around on him. When the air war failed to force Belgrade's capitulation, the Russians negotiated a settlement that allowed the U.S. and other NATO troops to enter and administer Kosovo. As part of that settlement, Russian troops were promised a significant part in peacekeeping in Kosovo. But the Russians were eventually shut out from that role, and Yeltsin proved unable to respond to the insult.

Were the knives out for Yeltsin? He thought so and called in the man that might be his successor, the youngest head of the FSB, the KGB's successor, only 43 when he was appointed, Vladimir Vladimirovich Putin. Though almost a child in the eyes of most Kremlin watchers, Putin was experienced in the politics of replacing heads of state in Russia, having taken the right side in the coup that almost replaced then-Soviet President Mikhail Gorbachev. Which side would he take on Yeltsin? All the high party members looked to him for guidance on how they should act.

Though privately, Putin was an admirer of Yeltsin for his ability to transition from the Soviet system to the smaller Russian Federation form, publicly, he emerged as the leading figure for a new direction for Russia, one that would make it more dominant again and to do it with by forceful means.

When Putin was seventeen years old and studying law, he also was pursuing interests in sports, wrestling and judo, mostly. He was told one morning after the class on Marxist doctrine that he was to take immediate action on his delinquency, which was his indifference to the finer points of Lenin's thought. His response? "I will do that, physically, as well as mentally, in order to take down my opponents."

Putin's mind went back to that incident when he was standing before Yeltsin while the Russian President was discussing details of the program for the International Peace Forum that was to be held in Moscow in two weeks. It was very important to the President that the forum go well, and it was Putin's job to see to it that there were no lapses in security.

Yeltsin looked tired and old as he talked, and a little drunk. Less drunk than he usually seemed, but more tired and old. "Vladimir, you are the most indispensable man I have. There cannot be any blemishes, none at all, at this event. Understand?"

"I do, my President, I understand fully," said Putin.

"Yes, I know you do. And I also know you won't let me down, as others have." Yeltsin picked up his cup of tea and took a quick swallow. *Was it spiked with Vodka this early in the day*, thought Putin?

"You have a fervent following, Vladimir, but so did I when I first took office. Keep that in mind when you are behind this desk." Then Yeltsin turned toward the picture of Lenin. "So did he, and so did many others, including Gorbachev, whom I replaced."

"But, my President, you are…

"I am the President now, but only now, so make your time count."

"I know what you have done for the country, and what you went through to achieve it," said Putin. "Dealing with idealists is sometimes worse that non-idealists, and insiders are worse than outsiders. Ambitions among the…." Putin stopped. Yeltsin was no longer listening. His eyes were partly closed and glassy-eyed, and his body slumped to his right side. Soon he would be snoring, and Putin thought it best to leave before that happened. Let someone else find him that way.

❖ ❖ ❖

"He wants to meet with someone 'in authority' to speak on behalf of America," said Bill Deutch to Bishop. "On what, he wouldn't say."

Bishop shook his head in disbelief.

"So he just, out of the blue, contacts the American Embassy and says he wants our help in killing Yeltsin?"

"Not exactly, but that was the inference. We knew about him and suspected he might be in on it."

Bishop nodded his head.

What Bishop knew about the plot to kill Yeltsin was that it wasn't an anti-Communist nor an ardent Communist faction this time, the two main motivations behind such plots, but personal revenge. And the man who had contacted the embassy was known to the CIA, Ivan Barochev, someone whose brother had been a general who paid the price for the last failed attempt to kill Yeltsin.

Bishop smelled a rat. Something was wrong about the situation, but he couldn't tell exactly what it was.
"Tell him straight away that you have someone to listen to his story, but can under no circumstances provide American help for any plots against the government," said Bishop. "Let's see what reaction that gets."

"And will you be the one to meet with him?"

"Of course."

"You, the guy who was most responsible for the death of his brother, want to sit down with him?"

"He doesn't know that."

"And you're willing to bet your life on it?"

"So, what else is new?"

"So, there's no definite time for the meeting?" Asked Bishop.

"That's the way he wants it," replied Bill Deutch. "He said it's for everyone's safety. 'Sometime late' is what he conveyed. And it's at a coffee bar, *Lizaveta*, that's open until two in the morning."

"And the paperback book *Crime and Punishment* by Dostoevsky is to be my identification?"

"Yes, and it should be held with two hands, Western-style, just in case anyone else has a copy of it there."

Bishop sighed. "You must know that Lizaveta was the name of the half-sister of the pawnbroker who is killed in the novel, someone who shows up in the wrong place at the wrong time and dies as well. Coincidence?"

"Tolstoy said all life and death is a coincidence." Replied Bill.

"Tolstoy led an aristocratic life, what would he know about 'all life and death'? And he scattered all his family members and sold off most of his possessions just before the 1905 Russian Revolution, which didn't come off as he expected. He was wrong about that as well. And for all his musings about family, his home life was a mess. He betrayed… He betrayed…."

"Pop," the name Bill used affectionately sometimes when speaking to his mentor even when he was not undercover with him, "betraying people who've leaned on us is bad stuff, very bad stuff, but it's what we do in our business. That's what you told me."

Bishop nodded his head in recognition of his own words.

"You've been dealing with things that sometimes meant life or death for yourself and our country for years. Communism was a threat to the U.S., to all of the West. This time we're dealing with lesser problems, but still serious ones. And the outcome is still important to us…"

"…Like the considerable implications of what Gorbachev started, and Yeltsin continued," added Bishop, repeating what he had said to Bill on their last assignment. *The kid heard me then,* thought Bishop, *and maybe the younger generation isn't going to let the world go to hell in a basket after all.*

◆ ◆ ◆

At *Lizaveta,* Bishop, his two hands firmly clutching a paperback copy of *Crime and Punishment,* gave the impression that he was focused intently on the novel, though he was also scanning the entire place simultaneously. A cup of coffee was to his right and a lit cigarette was in the ashtray to his left, from which he drew absent-mindedly from on occasion. A radio was on and playing soft violin sounds. About a dozen others were seated in the high-ceiled cafe that might have seated a hundred or more easily. A few minutes after midnight, Bishop heard the words, "I am Viktor."

The man was tall and thin, bearded, and wearing an overcoat that clearly was too large for him. He wore glasses and smelled of moss, wet moss. Bishop motioned him to sit down.

"I am Alan," said Bishop. "Alan Stanton. Do you want anything to eat or drink?"

"Yes, there is a buffet here, and I will take some cheese and bread. And, please join me in drinking some vodka."

Viktor walked away slowly, limping as he went.

When Viktor returned with his food, Bishop had already secured two glasses and a bottle of vodka. Viktor smiled and opened the bottle, pouring the vodka to the brim of each small glass. And, without waiting, he drank his down quickly and poured again.

"*Nostrovia!*" Viktor said, smiling a toothless smile, and then downed his Vodka again and poured another.

Time to get going on this, Bishop thought, *before he gets soused.* "I understand you have something to tell me."

"Yes, excuse my appearance, and my behavior, but I am dying... I know that. Just weeks maybe, or even days, but soon. But at least they gave me some more time. My brother was not so lucky. He was tortured mercilessly, and when they got tired of doing that, he was shot."

"Your brother was General Barochev?"

"Yes, they had him in a cell at the Lubyanka when they brought me in, my sister, and my mother. He was close to death then, and they wished to make him suffer more by bringing in his family. He didn't have a wife or children, so they brought us in because we were the next best thing. They —I say 'They,' but it was one man, Putin, who was handling it. I was there for many hours and pieced together what it was all about.

"Did Putin ever say what the charges were"

Viktor drank from his glass again. "Not exactly, but I figured it out. There was a conspiracy against Yeltsin, to kill and replace him. I don't know who else was involved, but my brother was, and he never divulged the names of anyone else."

"Did Putin ever mention any names to you?"

"Yes, he had a list, a long list, and kept going back to it to see if I reacted to any of them."

"Do you know any of them?"

Viktor took another drink, finishing the vodka, and poured another. "Not one... Except for my brother. He had told about his part in it, was even proud of it. But he would not say anything more. Yet they persisted, for days, to torture him with electricity, and cutting him. Then they started in on me."

Viktor looked at his glass of Vodka, downed it, and closed his eyes. "I am not like my brother. If I had known anything, I would have told them what they wanted to know. But I knew nothing, nothing at all, about the plot against the President. After some time, hours, maybe a day, they started in on our sister and mother — first one, then the other— there in the same room. They stripped them both and tied them down on chairs facing each other. Their time was shorter, maybe an hour each, but quite foul and offensive... The worse you can imagine. Of course, they didn't know anything, but they were tortured anyway. Then they left us alone in the room."

Viktor still had his eyes closed, but tears crept out of the edges.

"Was he able to talk to you? Did he say anything else?"
Viktor opened his eyes slowly, poured another drink, and downed it. "It was hard to make out what he was saying to me, but he wanted to tell me something. He used the English words 'ever' and 'stand.'"

Though Viktor had garbled the words, Bishop recognized them to mean Stan Evans, the name Bishop used in his last operation there in Russia.

"But that was all I could make out. I wanted to tell him that I would pledge to take up his cause, to do what I could do to assassinate the tyrant, but I didn't, of course, actually say it. There were obviously listening devices in the room. They'd have stood me up against the wall with my brother and shot us both."

Viktor looked at his food finally and started to eat rapidly; first bread, then cheese, more bread, then more cheese; always chewing and finishing each before taking another bite of the other.

"Look, Viktor, I am so sorry about what happened to your brother, you, and your family. But, I am here because I was told that you wanted to speak to someone from America who would help you kill Yeltsin. Is that right? Is there another plot against him? If so, I am here to tell you that under no circumstances would such aid be available. We were not involved in the last plot, nor will we be involved now."

"Are you telling me that your country did not have anything to do with the events involving my brother?"

Bishop thought for a moment, and then said, "I am here to tell you, from personal knowledge, that my government did not participate in any plot to kill Yeltsin."

Viktor seemed perplexed. "Your country was absolutely not involved? Is that true?"

"That is correct."

"Then why did my brother use English words to me? Were you involved in *stopping* it?"

Bishop looked indignant. "Where did you get that idea?" He fumed. "We work against your government, not with it."

Viktor drank again. "Yes, I know that. I am just trying to figure things out. Maybe I drink too much and say things I shouldn't. But you are here. To do what? If you cannot help me, will you betray me? Call someone and have me arrested? To keep me from taking a gun and killing the tyrant? Or Putin, or anyone I can?"

"I am here only to listen, and can do nothing else."

"I will talk no more. The vodka's finished, and so am I."

◆ ◆ ◆

Bishop's report to the President on his meeting with Viktor was brief: *There is no credible evidence of anything of substance to validate purpose of trip. Personal follow-up upon return.* It was marked Urgent and Personal, and placed on the President's reading list that day.

The President and First Lady had finished their simple dinner together and made their way to their sitting area. She sat on the sofa and started reading a magazine from a stack, finishing it by thumbing through it in under a minute, and then taking another. He put on the TV to a baseball game and started going through a file-full of reading items. She did not have dessert; he did and asked for a second helping of apple pie with ice cream that he brought with him to the sitting area. He placed it close to him so that he could take bites as he went through his reading and also keep an eye on the game, Atlanta versus Baltimore, two of his favorite teams.

"Well, this is good news!" He said.

"What is? Did Newt Gingrich die? If not, there's no reason why you should get apple pie on the rug… Careful now… Shit! You can't even eat your dessert without getting some of it on you."

"It'll come off. You act like you have to do it yourself.

"I do a heck of a lot here, why not that?"

"I know you do. And we're in it together, the way it's always been."

"No, some things you do without me, and that's when you get into trouble."

Bill's glasses were well down his nose, and lowering his gaze toward Hillary when she said that, they started to slip off. "Damn these! I need a new pair."

"I've got two bigger than yours," said Hillary.

"The biggest in D.C., by far." Bill quipped.

"And don't you forget it!"

"How can I when you remind me of it daily."

They both laughed.

"OK, what is it?" Said the First Lady.

"I'm not going to tell you now."

"Suit yourself."

"And maybe I will tell you… Though I really shouldn't."

"Again, do what you want to do. If it's important, I'll read about it later in the Times. If not, it'll be on Fox."

"What if it never appears on both?"

"There are no trees that fall in the D.C. forest that don't make a sound. Someone always hears them."

◆ ◆ ◆

Something still nagged at Bishop. Was Viktor just a lure? He certainly wasn't a threat to Yeltsin or anyone else. Maybe a meeting with Putin that Darrow sought would shed some light on it? Darrow had struck out with the Russian lawyer he had contacted previously, and two others as well. No one wanted any part of a lawsuit filed by an American lawyer, even if he was representing a

Nobel Prize-winning Russian scientist. He and Darrow had spent two days at the Lubyanka trying to get a meeting with Putin; maybe a third day would be the charm.

The previous week in which Darrow and he made the rounds of the legal establishment, the cultural offices, the ministries of publishing and related agencies, and visiting dozens of officials, from minor office holders to heads of departments brought to mind the question that always haunted him: how was it that the Soviet Union, and now the Russian Federation, could economically afford what it sponsored? The sports establishment, the space race, the arts, and the military, on what most economists estimated was on par with the economies of Norway or Chile.

The offices they visited of even ministry heads were usually small and austere, windowless and dank, no larger than work stations of clerks in the U.S. And the responses always seemed to be, "We will have to refer that to higher up." Passing the buck was the easy solution for evading responsibility for any problem, no matter what it was. Maybe *perestroika* and *glasnost* hadn't made their way to the bureaucracy. Certainly it had not penetrated the Lubyanka.

Lubyanka, the former headquarters and prison of the KGB, and still used by its successor, the FSB, was only a twenty-minute walk from Bishop's hotel. And he found himself there many nights looking at the fortress where terrible people had done so much to hurt so many.

During those walking visits, Bishop reflected on some of the victims he had known and worked with personally, and occasionally helped. He thought back on his almost forty-year career in the spy business of his country and how diligently he and others had worked to frustrate the enemy, so productively engaged, for so long, in its myriad enterprises, including death for millions, misery for other millions, laboring always to penetrate the defenses of the Western world, whether by actual or hypothetical weapons, or by electronic stealth. Or, with a terrible record of success, by the seduction of individual Westerners.

Academics and scientists were major targets, including several that found their way to the Manhattan Project, funneling its secrets to Stalin. Hollywood and the press were lesser targets, but many times more fruitful in numbers and influence. Even the intelligence community was targeted, with many infiltrators found in the CIA, and the head of the British equivalent, MI6, Kim Philby, revealed to be a Soviet double agent.

Would this present mission be his last? He was feeling tired too often lately. In body and spirit? More the latter now than the former. Already he had surmised that the threat of assassination and coup against Yeltsin was remote and communicated that to the President. There was nothing more to do, but carry out the pretense of his cover story with Darrow and meet with Putin.

Bishop would keep his cover, and, no doubt, so would Putin. That's what spies did, on both sides.

Of course, that meeting would be non-productive because it was Putin who was behind the republishing of Natalia Bakitsa's books, enriching himself. That was quickly learned by Bishop after he got Bill Deutch to investigate the paper trail of royalties that flowed through numerous banks across several countries to Putin's accounts in Bulgaria. The KGB's installation of that country's former king to power, after turning him into an agent of theirs, assured the KGB of having their own banking system free of even Soviet or Russian government interference.

Putin's last communication with Bishop came to mind, one in which he said, *Feel free to drop in and see me anytime you are in Moscow. And if you want to finally turn against your country, I will be a most helpful host in that regard. You already know I can persuade anyone considering defection to take my side. And you know I am schooled in how to conceal allegiances.*

Bishop had several drinks this evening and maybe his feelings were intensified by them. His fist went smash against the street lamp and ripped open his best leather gloves.

"Damn!" He said under his breath, and then looked around to see if anyone else had witnessed one of the few times he let his emotions take charge.

Bishop remembered the events that brought so much anger and frustration to mind. It started with a letter from Natalia Bakitsa to the Soviet Ambassador for France back in 1989, when Natalia was attending a scientific conference in Paris. It was a long letter that recounted dozens of problems she was having in her lab back home having to do with supplies, funding, equipment, and research material, as well as the inability to freely communicate with her counterparts in other countries.

She ended the letter, "I have reflected that it is not possible for me to continue my work in the repressive Soviet Union. Accordingly, I have resolved to leave Moscow and take up residence in the United States. But in recognition of my Russian blood and of my love for my motherland, I am amendable to accommodation. If it can be arranged to transport my past work and my archives to Paris, I will undertake to continue my work here without a formal estrangement. You will need to arrange for two of my associates, Luzhin and Paval, to join me. I have been assured by persons here that technical resources are available, but in their absence, I expect Moscow to arrange to provide whatever I request be shipped to me, materials or sufficient funds that I will itemize if we agree to proceed. I expect a response within three days. If that is not forthcoming, I will assume the decision is negative as to any accommodation."

The letter set off occurrences in both capitals. In Moscow, the ministers of Foreign Affairs, Culture, and Science were summoned by the Deputy Chairman. After the usual recriminations and expressions of outrage —"I cannot imagine anything so grotesque... A traitor to the homeland that nurtured her... We must find who else took part in this."— it was noted that the letter made no ideological statements or repudiation of the Communist cause. Her complaints were specific and personal to her work. It was decided that an effort would be made to induce her to remain. And that to persuade her, they must assign their best.

"Their best," it was decided by Moscow, was the man who had just arrived there from East Germany for a new assignment, Vladimir Putin. And in Washington, the hastily convened meeting of the Secretary of State, the Vice President and the head of the CIA decided that the best man to counter Putin was his opposite number in East Germany for almost a decade, Ambrose Bishop.

"I know the man," said Bishop to the CIA Director when he was given the assignment, "better than I've ever known anyone else, including my wife, and there isn't anyone I'd rather not face. He gets his way, or busts his ass trying."

Then CIA Director William Webster, a no-nonsense type who headed the FBI before being appointed to the CIA post, said to Bishop, "Then accommodate him —bust his ass, but get that scientist to defect."

◆ ◆ ◆

Bishop met Natalia Bakitsa at the Ritz Hotel in Paris for lunch and found her to be egotistical, pompous and demanding, even condescending, which he thought might be an asset in prevailing upon her to come to America. Seated in one of the booths, with the finest crystal stemware and patterned silver on the table, and the rich red velvet and the gilt scrunches over each of the carved-wood booths, she didn't seem a likely candidate to return to the Soviet Union and its repressive system.

The Russians had responded and asked for a meeting of both sides to "discuss" the matter. Natalia agreed. The meeting would take place in a conference room of the Ritz, with each side able to hear and counter what the other said. And each side had one opportunity to meet alone with her, but publicly, beforehand. The Russian meeting would be that night for dinner.

"Is it not true that Soviet citizens who have defected to America have found less than ideal lives there?" Natalia said to Bishop upon sitting.

"Ideal? You mean, what the Russian Constitution envisions," Bishop responded. "Or what reality is in both countries?"

"I mean what Boris Kirov found to be the case after he moved there: isolation, almost no personal life, frequent moves, and limited travel."

"Kirov defected almost twenty years ago and feared for his life until recently. Those were different times, with restrictions needed for his sake. Now, things are different for scientists, more on par with artists who had no such concerns for safety."

"It is so," replied Natalia, and said no more about it during the lunch, which began with Tuna Tartare, followed by Salmon, accompanied by Provence rosè and champagne, both Baron De Rothschild.

And that was the last Bishop saw of Natalia. After her dinner meeting with Putin, she checked out of the hotel and left immediately for Moscow. Why? Bishop could only speculate. "They got to her somehow," Bishop said to Webster. "Whatever Putin threatened her with made the difference. *What was it?* Your guess is as good as mine. But it must have been big. This time they didn't need a KGB kidnapping to get her out of Paris; she returned on her own."

The Natalia Bakitsa defection incident never became public because either side wanted it leaked to the press. The Russians saw nothing good in publicizing any attempt to defect no matter the eventual outcome. Certainly, the Americans didn't because they failed to land her. And the blame was placed on Bishop, the low point in his almost forty year career with the CIA.

For all Bishop had done over the years, operating in several theaters winning the respect of his colleagues and superiors, and even some of his adversaries, what he was most remembered by was the Bakitsa defection. And no matter how many assignments, small or significant, that he took on and completed successfully, it was never enough to scrub his failure for that one blown mission.

◆ ◆ ◆

As planned, Darrow met Bishop at the hotel restaurant of the Regent Hotel. Bishop was reading a paperback and smiled, not mentioning that Darrow was almost a half-hour late.

"Let's order immediately," said Bishop. "I'm famished."

"So am I," said Darrow. "It's the same menu each night, so I think I already know what I want… the beef."

They were about to get their waiter's attention when the headwaiter came to their table with an ice bucket and a bottle of Dom Pérignon champagne.

"Mr. Bishop, this bottle was ordered to be served to you with this card."

Darrow looked at Bishop. "Who is Bishop?"

Darrow opened the note, which was in Russian. Something clicked in Darrow's mind. He handed it to Bishop and said, "It must be for you… Bishop."

Bishop ran his eyes over the note and immediately recognized Putin's writing. The note read: "You are persistent, and this will be rewarded. You may come at ten tomorrow for a reunion. Perhaps your last meeting with me or anyone else in Russia.”

After Bishop told Darrow about the meeting, he replied, “Lucy, *Bishop*, or whatever your name is, you have some splainin to do!”

◆ ◆ ◆

At the front of the Lubyanya were two armed guards that met Bishop and Darrow, and checked their identities. The guards then accompanied them through a series of check-points to what appeared to be one of the most well-guarded places on earth, Putin’s private office. Bishop had told Darrow the previous night that he was with the CIA and knew Putin, but not why he was there. Only that he was on assignment, and it was happenstance that they got together. Darrow accepted it, but didn’t believe it. No matter, he was going to see Putin after all.

It was a fine sunny day, and the light filtering in through the iron bars enveloped the room. The walls had been freshly painted as there was a hint of fresh paint in the air. Putin was sitting behind a massive desk cleared of everything but a phone. The composition of the room hadn’t changed much over the years, through the administrations of Stalin and Khruschchev, Brezhnev and Andropov, Chernenko and Gorbachev, and now Yeltsin. Each had their paintings placed along side the other two that remained constant: Marx and Lenin.

Putin opened by saying, “Why do you want to meet with me so badly, Mr. Darrow? Did you think I could be of some service with your client’s problems? I know of them, of course, but why did you think I could help?

“You could if you wanted to. And you know that.”

"I am just a civil servant in my country, nothing more," said Putin.

"You are the most important person in the country, even, at this time, more important than the General Secretary and President."

"Your companion knows otherwise," said Putin. "He knows everything… Or so he thinks."

"I know a lot," said Bishop. "But not why you're the one stealing from Natalia about a million rubles a year? What's that, maybe 35 to 40 thousand dollars a year tops? You could just let her publish and make double that by taking a small percentage."

"You presume too much, my friend," said Putin, eyeing Darrow's reaction. "Too much in what you say, and in our previous alliance of convenience."

"Wasn't it enough that you got her to return to the fold, back in harness and working for the Soviet Union? That's probably one of the reasons why you're sitting behind that desk. Sure, he gets perks and recognition, but not the money she's due from her work, not yours. She got the Nobel Prize, for Christ's sake, you didn't… Or did you?"

The epiphany came to Bishop and almost floored him.

"That's it, isn't it? You gave her the Nobel Prize. It wasn't a threat you made that got her to return. You didn't take into custody any family members, you didn't have to. You just promised to give her the one thing she wanted most of all… The Nobel Prize!"

Putin's smile could not be contained. It came through even though he tried hard not to let his delight in Bishop finally recognizing his achievement be visible.

"Son of a bitch! I knew it. And what did it cost you? Not much, I suspect. Them Swedes have been selling it for years."

"What it cost me was worth it, in value to my country and to me. And to have you suffer as a result was also useful."

What will you do now that your secret will be revealed?

"This is what I will do, Bishop," said Putin, pistol in hand.
Two shots rang out, hitting Bishop in the heart and forehead, placed precisely where Putin intended. From the ground, he attempted to speak, but Putin walked over and put a third bullet into his mouth.

Darrow knelt beside the body and checked Bishop. He could feel no pulse waited, immobile, until Putin said, "This was longstanding, and had to come to an end this way. As to you, you will get what you wanted for your client. You can tell her that you have cleared it with me that she will get all her royalties in the future. Those in the past? Well, those are gone, forever. But the Nobel Prize is still hers, and will remain that way forever."

MOVIE NIGHT AT THE WHITE HOUSE WITH JFK, JACKIE AND FRIENDS

Our viewing habits can tell quite a lot about us, including occupants of the White House

There were just the two of them that night to see a movie in the family theater wing of the White House, John F. Kennedy and his wife Jackie, and they sat apart, he on his rocking chair off to the right of the assembled chairs, and she front row center. In between was a small table where snacks were placed for them; thin ginger cookies and tea for her, and wine and cheese for him.

"You may not like the movie tonight, but give it more than five minutes —at best ten minutes to be certain before you get up and leave," said John.

"With that kind of description, maybe I should leave now so you can enjoy it by yourself," she said, half serious. "There's no one else here to take some political significance or personal meaning from what I do."

JFK wrinkled his brow and, ignoring that remark, said, "You've got to hear this about the movie. But I won't say anything to give the plot away."

"Why say anything at all then?"

JFK wrinkled his brow even further.

Jackie sighed, and then said, "OK. Come on, honey, What is it about?"

JFK smiled and said, "It's *From Russia With Love*, the second James Bond film. I read the book and it's better than the first book and film. It's the craziest plot I've ever read about spies and the Cold War, and the most exciting. This beautiful Russian girl gets a crush on Bond and…"

"I thought you weren't going to give away the plot?"

"Well, not the plot exactly, just the highlights of what's going on. Anyway, there's this beautiful doll of a girl who's been recruited to lure Bond to his death, and she's Russian, working for SPECTRE, but thinks she's still working for the Russians, but secretly wants to defect to the British because of her attraction to Bond. Crazy, huh? And all this takes place in Turkey, where there's gypsies, and spies on both sides, the U.S. included, and Bulgarians, and SPECTRE, of course, with their Number 1, 2, 3, and 4 all a part of it. And, you'll like this, Number 3 is Lotte Lenya, mentioned in Mack the Knife!"

JFK's eyes were wide in delight.

"With all that, I don't need to see the movie. You told me everything that's going to happen.

"No, just the big picture. The actual plot is…"

Just then, a group of people enter from the back. Among them,

Peter Lawford and his wife Patricia, JFK's sister. Peter had last been there when the movie *Misfits* was shown. Peter had been John's connection to Hollywood, and many of Hollywood's leading ladies and starlets alike, including Marilyn Monroe, the star of *Misfits*.

It had been an agonizing experience for Jackie that night, sitting through the movie and picturing her husband with Marilyn in all the scenes. She thought she had left Peter's name off the guest list for all future showings of movies at the White House, but he showed up somehow.

"I heard that the latest James Bond movie was on tonight and rounded up some friends," said Peter. "I hope you don't mind, folks.

"Not at all, Peter," said JFK. "Especially if you have Joey Bishop and his lovely bridge Sylvia with you, and... Is that Charles Nelson Reilly with you?"

"YO!" Reilly said in a loud, deep voice. "IN PERSON!"

Then, as if Reilly realized he wasn't on camera, less loudly said, "Fresh off my Tony Award-winning performance as Bud in the Pulitzer prize-winning musical *How to Succeed in Business Without Really Trying*.

Jackie thought back to when they first started seeing movies in the White House. It was just the two of them for the most part, and they enjoyed viewing such films as *Paris Blues* starring Paul Newman and Joanne Woodward, and *Blood and Roses*, a French film that she enjoyed because she spoke French. Some movies though, such as *Sergeants Three* and *The Guns of Navarone* were "guy films," and many others showed up to see them. She left as discretely as she could soon after they began.

Turning toward JKF, Jackie said, in a whisper, "Your Hollywood buddies are here now and can keep you company while I disappear. Don't worry, there's no one in the crowd who'll take offense or political signal from it."

JFK lost all his color. "Well, if you really want to leave, that's fine. They're filming the next Bond movie now. It's called *Goldfinger*. Maybe you can read the book first, so you can be ready for it when it's released. It's about someone who is obsessed with gold and what it can buy. You can relate to that, can't you?"

ABOUT THE AUTHOR

John Corral

He is an award-winning author of mysteries, thrillers, suspense, legal dramas, and westerns. John Corral also co-wrote and edited women's stories of love and life with Tanya Angel, and contributed and edited poetry with Ian Lewis and Iris Mede.

Books by the author include SERIAL SINS OF SIBERIA, LUST, LIES, AND LOVE, GETTING SADDAM'S GOLD, LOVE TIMES ELEVEN, THE GRISLY EFFECTS OF GREEN, HIS FINAL RESTING PLACE: ELVIS, REDHEADS ARE RELENTLESS, DELPHINA: VOODOO QUEEN, 30 FLASHES OF FICTION, 15 FLASHES OF FICTION, 15 MORE FLASHES OF FICTION, MYSTERY AND MALICE, IMPERFECT KILLING, PROSECUTION MISCONDUCT, REMEMBERING DIXIE, BEYOND THERE BE DRAGONS and THE MOST DANGEROUS MAN IN THE WORLD.

Books with Tanya Angel include THE SECRET LIVES OF SMILES, THE DUCHESS, WHERE THE HEART IS, and WHEN THE HEART LAUGHS IT SHOW AND WHEN IT DOESN'T IT SHOWS EVEN MORE.

Books with Ian Lewis and Iris Mede include FLOWING LIQUID LIFE, DREAMS OF A PERPETUAL DREAMER, EVOLVING LOVE, LET LOVE FLOAT, ORDINARY LIVES EXTRAORDINARY LOVES, LET

LOVE LEAD THE WAY, REAL PASSIONS REAL LOVE, LOVE THAT CHANGES EVERYTHING, THE SENSE OF SORROWS PAST, LOVE DEVILISH LOVE DIVINE, TALKING DIRTY ABOUT DESIRE, LOVE WORTH REMEMBERING, THE PLEASURES AND PAIN OF LOVE, WHEN LOVE LIFTS YOU HIGH, and WHEN LOVE SIZZLES.

John is also the author of TWO BROTHERS, a western, 3 LIFE LES-SONS, an essay, and SEEING YOU, a book of poetry.